For more information, please contact:
Mascot Books
560 Herndon Parkway #120
Herndon, VA 20170
info@mascotbooks.com

CPSIA Code: PRT1113A
ISBN-10: 1620864819
ISBN-13: 9781620864814

Printed in the United States

Hello, Baxter The Bobcat!™

Naren Aryal
Illustrated by Danny Moore

It was a beautiful day in Phoenix, Arizona.
Baxter The Bobcat was on his way to the ballpark for a baseball game.

As he walked through the city, *Diamondbacks* fans cheered,
"Hello, *Baxter The Bobcat*!"

The mascot was so excited to be going to the game, and couldn't wait to watch his favorite team play.

In front of the ballpark, he ran into lots of *Diamondbacks* fans.
They cheered, "Hello, *Baxter The Bobcat*!"

Baxter The Bobcat arrived on the field just in time for batting practice. Each player took swings to get ready for the game.

As the team's best hitter stepped to home plate,
he said, "Hello, *Baxter The Bobcat*!"

After batting practice, the grounds crew
proudly prepared the field for play.

As the grounds crew worked, they hollered,
"Hello, *Baxter The Bobcat!*"

Baxter The Bobcat was feeling hungry. He grabbed a few snacks and a *Diamondbacks* pennant at the concession stand.

As he made his way back to the field,
a family shouted, "Hello, *Baxter The Bobcat!*"

Each *Diamondbacks* player stood on the first-base line
as the home team was introduced.

Baxter received the largest applause!
Fans roared, "Hello, *Baxter The Bobcat*!"

"PLAY BALL!" yelled the umpire. The *Diamondbacks* pitcher delivered a fastball to start the game. "STRIKE ONE!" called the umpire.

The umpire noticed the mascot nearby and said,
"Hello, *Baxter The Bobcat!*"

Baxter The Bobcat went into the bleachers to visit his fans.
Everyone was excited to see him.

A family waved and called out, "Hello, *Baxter The Bobcat!*"

It was now time for the seventh inning stretch. The mascot led the crowd as everyone sang "Take Me Out To The Ballgame™!"

Young *Diamondbacks* fans danced on the dugout with
Baxter The Bobcat. They cheered, "Let's go, *Diamondbacks*!"

In the bottom of the ninth inning, a *Diamondbacks* player hit a game-winning home run over the right-field fence.

The team gathered at home plate to celebrate the victory.
The players chanted, "*Diamondbacks* win, *Diamondbacks* win!"

After the game, *Baxter The Bobcat* was tired. It had been a long day at the ballpark. He walked home and went straight to bed.

Goodnight, *Baxter The Bobcat*!

Have a book idea?

Contact us at:

Mascot Books
560 Herndon Parkway #120
Herndon, VA 20170

info@mascotbooks.com | www.mascotbooks.com

™